Please Don't Laugh, I Can Use a Graph!

Esther Beck

Consulting Editors, Diane Craig, M.A./Reading Specialist
and Susan Kosel, M.A. Education

Published by ABDO Publishing Company, 4940 Viking Drive, Edina, Minnesota 55435.

Printed in the United States.

Credits
Edited by: Pam Price
Curriculum Coordinator: Nancy Tuminelly
Cover and Interior Design and Production: Mighty Media
Photo Credits: Brand X Pictures, Comstock, Photodisc, ShutterStock, Thinkstock, TongRo Image Stock,
Wewerka Photography

Library of Congress Cataloging-in-Publication Data

Beck, Esther.
    Please don't laugh, I can use a graph! / Esther Beck.
    p. cm. -- (Science made simple)
    ISBN 10 1-59928-614-9 (hardcover)
    ISBN 10 1-59928-615-7 (paperback)

    ISBN 13 978-1-59928-614-3 (hardcover)
    ISBN 13 978-1-59928-615-0 (paperback)
    1. Graph theory--Juvenile literature. I. Title.

QA166.B34 2007
511'.5--dc22

                                                        2006022590

SandCastle Level: Transitional

SandCastle™ books are created by a professional team of educators, reading specialists, and content developers around
five essential components—phonemic awareness, phonics, vocabulary, text comprehension, and fluency—to assist young
readers as they develop reading skills and strategies and increase their general knowledge. All books are written,
reviewed, and leveled for guided reading, early reading intervention, and Accelerated Reader® programs for use in
shared, guided, and independent reading and writing activities to support a balanced approach to literacy instruction.
The SandCastle™ series has four levels that correspond to early literacy development. The levels help teachers and
parents select appropriate books for young readers.

| **Emerging Readers** | **Beginning Readers** | **Transitional Readers** | **Fluent Readers** |
| (no flags) | (1 flag) | (2 flags) | (3 flags) |

These levels are meant only as a guide. All levels are subject to change.

A **graph** is a drawing that shows how two or more things are related. Graphs, tables, and charts help us organize and understand information.

Words used to talk about graphs:
chart
pictograph
table
tally chart

I keep a tally chart of the I put in my .

August

Pennies	Nickels	Dimes	Quarters	Half-Dollars
卌 卌 l	ll	llll	卌 ll	ll

We make a graph to record how high the bounces when dropped from different heights.

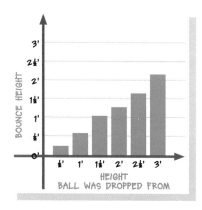

I like to 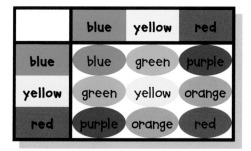 . I make a table that shows the result when I mix two colors. and make !

	blue	yellow	red
blue	blue	green	purple
yellow	green	yellow	orange
red	purple	orange	red

At the zoo, we count the

legs of each animal.

Then we make a graph.

The has eight legs!

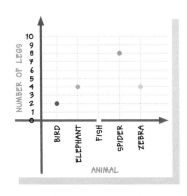

The class makes a pictograph to count who likes vanilla and who likes strawberry.

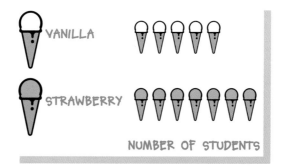

VANILLA

STRAWBERRY

NUMBER OF STUDENTS

The graph of my pets shows one , two , three and one 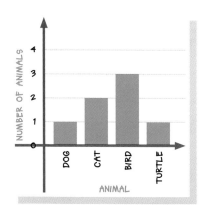 .

Please Don't Laugh, I Can Use a Graph!

Marie is busy as can be, reading books for a contest at the library. Her friend Sophia laughs, "Why are you making a silly graph?"

No worries!
It's time to show
Sophia everything
I know.

11

BOOKS I'VE READ THIS SUMMER

ANDY

CHRIS

LIZ

MARIE

MIKE

PAM

"Look here, if you please,"
Marie says with ease.
A pile of books is
stacked to her knees.
"A graph helps me track
what I have done,
so I can see if I've won!"

I think it's really cool to use what I have learned in school!

BOOKS I'VE READ THIS SUMMER

ANDY 📚📚📚
CHRIS 📚📚📚📚📚
LIZ 📚📚📚📚
MARIE 📚📚📚📚📚📚📚📚
MIKE 📚📚📚
PAM 📚📚📚

When the contest ends,
Marie shows the prize
to her friend.
Sophia says,
"Good job, Marie.
Graphs are great!
Will you teach me?"

Why not?
Graphs are fun.
I think I'll make
another one!

15

Graphs Every Day!

Thomas and his friends make a graph with everyone's name and height.

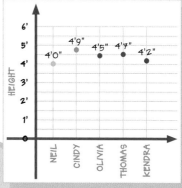

Look on the graph to see who is the tallest!

HEIGHT

6'
5'
4'
3'
2'
1'

4'0"   4'9"   4'5"   4'7"   4'2"

NEIL   CINDY   OLIVIA   THOMAS   KENDRA

17

Amber keeps a chart of the number of hours she practices the piano each week.

Practice makes perfect!

NUMBER OF HOURS PRACTICED	1	1½	0	¾	1	0	2
	SUNDAY	MONDAY	TUESDAY	WEDNESDAY	THURSDAY	FRIDAY	SATURDAY

We count the number of letters in our first names and make a **tally chart**.

I have four letters in my name.

Keiko	Li
卌	‖
Michael	Ryan
卌 ‖	‖‖

Jude's grandfather is a gardener. He records whether or not it rains each day.

What other kinds of weather information could you show on a graph?

RAIN		X			X		X X
NO RAIN			X	X		X	
		SUNDAY	MONDAY	TUESDAY	WEDNESDAY	THURSDAY	FRIDAY	SATURDAY

Glossary

chart – information presented in a form such as a table or graph.

information – the facts known about an event or subject.

pictograph – a graph that uses pictures to show amounts. You count the pictures to total the amounts.

table – an organized list of facts.

tally – to keep count. You can make tally marks on a tally chart to record how often something happens.